MICHAEL FOREMAN'S
CHRISTMAS TREASURY

MICHAEL FOREMAN'S
CHRISTMAS TREASURY

PAVILION

First published in Great Britain in 1999 by
PAVILION BOOKS LIMITED
London House, Great Eastern Wharf
Parkgate Road, London SW11 4NQ

Illustrations © Michael Foreman 1999
Introduction, Afterword and text selection
© Michael Foreman 1999
For text credits, please refer to page 124
Design and layout © Pavilion Books Ltd. 1999

The moral right of the authors and illustrator
has been asserted

Designed by Janet James

A CIP catalogue record for this book is available
from the British Library.

ISBN 1 86205 197 6

Set in Caslon 540

Colour origination by DP Reprographics, England
Printed and bound in Spain by Bookprint

2 4 6 8 10 9 7 5 3

This book can be ordered direct from the publisher. Please contact
the Marketing Department. But try your bookshop first.

CONTENTS

 INTRODUCTION

It is Christmas Eve. I can hear carols drift across the harbour and the white lights of a Christmas tree dance on the water. High above the dark town, the brightly lit cross on the church tower seems to float in the air like a star.

My wife and children are downstairs, and I remember another Christmas Eve, long ago, when again I was upstairs and everyone downstairs. It was a very big family that year, a family of many nations. French, Polish, Canadian, Czech and Scots, soldiers, sailors, airmen all gathered around our table playing cards. Other children's fathers, far from home and on their way to war. For some, this was their last Christmas.

They all kissed me goodnight and my mother carried me upstairs to bed. I went to sleep to the sound of laughter and some singing and when the sleigh bells came I did not hear them.

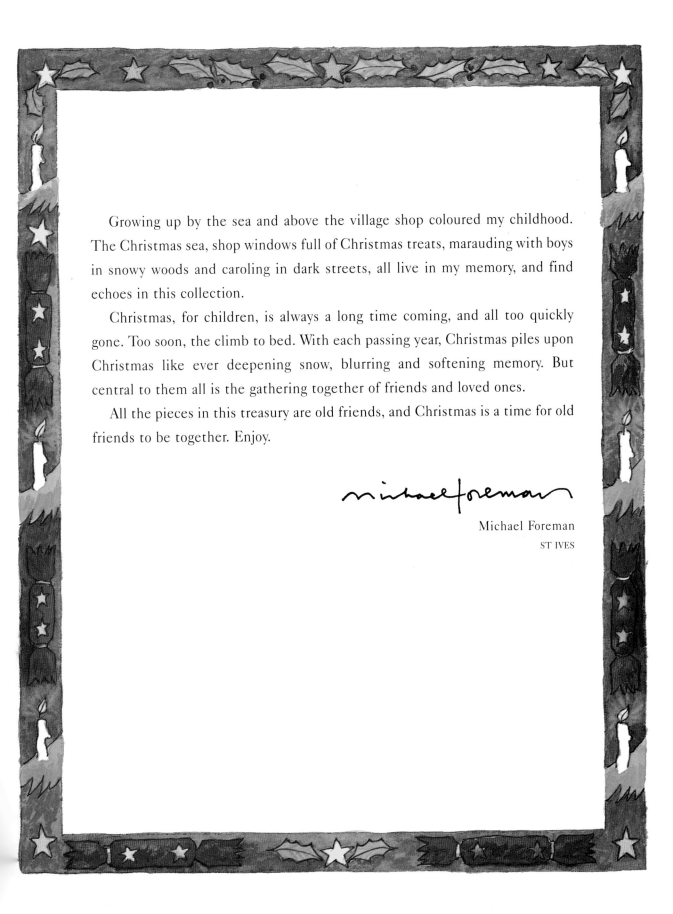

Growing up by the sea and above the village shop coloured my childhood. The Christmas sea, shop windows full of Christmas treats, marauding with boys in snowy woods and caroling in dark streets, all live in my memory, and find echoes in this collection.

Christmas, for children, is always a long time coming, and all too quickly gone. Too soon, the climb to bed. With each passing year, Christmas piles upon Christmas like ever deepening snow, blurring and softening memory. But central to them all is the gathering together of friends and loved ones.

All the pieces in this treasury are old friends, and Christmas is a time for old friends to be together. Enjoy.

Michael Foreman
ST IVES

Picture-Books in Winter

Robert Louis Stevenson

Summer fading, winter comes –
Frosty mornings, tingling thumbs,
Window robins, winter rocks,
And the picture story-books.

Water now is turned to stone
Nurse and I can walk upon;
Still we find the flowing brooks
In the picture story-books.

All the pretty things put by,
Wait upon the children's eye,
Sheep and shepherds, trees and crooks,
In the picture story-books.

We may see how all things are,
Seas and cities, near and far,
And the flying fairies' looks,
In the picture story-books.

How am I to sing your praise,
Happy chimney-corner days,
Sitting safe in nursery nooks,
Reading picture story-books?

The Twelve Days of Christmas

Traditional

On the first day of Christmas,
My true love sent to me
A partridge in a pear tree.

The second day of Christmas,
My true love sent to me
Two turtledoves, and
A partridge in a pear tree.

The third day of Christmas,
My true love sent to me
Three French hens,
Two turtledoves, and
A partridge in a pear tree.

The fourth day of Christmas,
My true love sent to me
Four colly birds,
Three French hens,
Two turtledoves, and
A partridge in a pear tree.

The fifth day of Christmas,
My true love sent to me
Five gold rings,
Four colly birds,
Three French hens,
Two turtledoves, and
A partridge in a pear tree.

The sixth day of Christmas,
My true love sent to me
Six geese a-laying,
Five gold rings,
Four colly birds,
Three French hens,
Two turtledoves, and
A partridge in a pear tree.

The seventh day of Christmas,
My true love sent to me
Seven swans a-swimming,
Six geese a-laying,
Five gold rings,
Four colly birds,
Three French hens,
Two turtledoves, and
A partridge in a pear tree.

The eighth day of Christmas,
My true love sent to me
Eight maids a-milking,
Seven swans a-swimming,
Six geese a-laying,
Five gold rings,
Four colly birds,
Three French hens,
Two turtledoves, and
A partridge in a pear tree.

The ninth day of Christmas,
My true love sent to me
Nine drummers drumming,
Eight maids a-milking,
Seven swans a-swimming,
Six geese a-laying,
Five gold rings,
Four colly birds,
Three French hens,
Two turtledoves, and
A partridge in a pear tree.

The tenth day of Christmas,
My true love sent to me
Ten pipers piping,
Nine drummers drumming,
Eight maids a-milking,
Seven swans a-swimming,
Six geese a-laying,
Five gold rings,
Four colly birds,
Three French hens,
Two turtledoves, and
A partridge in a pear tree.

The eleventh day of Christmas,
My true love sent to me
Eleven ladies dancing,
Ten pipers piping,
Nine drummers drumming,
Eight maids a-milking,
Seven swans a-swimming,
Six geese a-laying,
Five gold rings,
Four colly birds,
Three French hens,
Two turtledoves, and
A partridge in a pear tree.

The twelth day of Christmas,
My true love sent to me
Twelve lords a-leaping,
Eleven ladies dancing,
Ten pipers piping,
Nine drummers drumming,
Eight maids a-milking,
Seven swans a-swimming,
Six geese a-laying,
Five gold rings,
Four colly birds,
Three French hens,
Two turtledoves, and
A partridge in a pear tree.

Good King Wenceslas

Traditional

Good King Wenceslas looked out,
On the Feast of Stephen,
When the snow lay round about,
Deep and crisp and even;
Brightly shone the moon that night,
Though the frost was cruel,
When a poor man came in sight,
Gath'ring winter fuel.

'Hither page, and stand by me,
If thou knowst it, telling,
Yonder peasant, who is he?
Where and what his dwelling?'
'Sire, he lives a good league hence,
Underneath the mountain,
Right against the forest fence,
By Saint Agnes' fountain.'

'Bring me flesh and bring me wine,
Bring me pine logs hither:
Thou and I will see him dine,
When we bear them thither.'
Page and monarch forth they went,
Forth they went together
Through the rude wind's wild lament
And the bitter weather.

'Sire, the night is darker now,
And the wind blows stronger;
Fails my heart, I know not how;
I can go no longer.'
'Mark my footsteps, good my page,
Tread thou in them boldly;
Thou shalt find the winter's rage
Freeze they blood less coldly.'

In his master's steps he trod,
Where the snow lay dinted;
Heat was in the very sod
Which the Saint had printed.
Therefore, Christian men, be sure,
Wealth or rank possessing,
Ye who now will bless the poor,
Shall yourselves find blessing.

ON THE PRAIRIE

Extract from *Little House in the Big Woods*
Laura Ingalls Wilder

Christmas was coming.

The little log house was almost buried in snow. Great drifts were banked against the walls and windows, and in the morning when Pa opened the door, there was a wall of snow as high as Laura's head. Pa took the shovel and shovelled it away, and then he shovelled a path to the barn, where the horses and cows were snug and warm in their stalls.

The days were clear and bright. Laura and Mary stood on chairs by the window and looked out across the glittering snow at the glittering trees. Snow was piled all along their bare, dark branches, and it sparkled in the sunshine. Icicles hung from the caves of the house to the snow-banks, great icicles as large at the top as Laura's arm. They were like glass and full of sharp lights.

Pa's breath hung in the air like smoke, when he came along the path from the barn. He breathed it out in clouds and it froze in white frost on his moustache and beard.

When he came in, stamping the snow from his boots, and caught Laura up in a bear's hug against his cold, big coat, his moustache was beaded with little drops of melting frost. Every night he was busy, working on a large piece of board and two small pieces. He whittled them with his knife, he rubbed them with sandpaper and with the palm of his hand, until when Laura touched them they felt soft and smooth as silk.

Then with his sharp jack-knife he worked at them, cutting the edges of the large one into little peaks and towers, with a large star curved on the very tallest point. He cut little holes through the wood. He cut the holes in shapes of windows, and little stars, and crescent moons, and circles. All around them he carved tiny leaves, and flowers, and birds.

One of the little boards he shaped in a lovely curve, and around its edges he carved leaves and flowers and stars, and through it he cut crescent moons and curlicues.

Around the edges of the smallest board he carved a tiny flowering vine.

He made the tiniest shavings, cutting very slowly and carefully, making whatever he thought would be pretty.

At last he had the pieces finished and one night he fitted them together. When this was done, the large piece was a beautifully carved back for a smooth little shelf across its middle. The large star was at the very top of it. The curved piece supported the shelf underneath, and it was carved beautifully, too. And the little vine ran around the edge of the shelf.

Pa had made this bracket for a Christmas present for Ma. He hung it carefully against the log wall between the windows, and Ma stood her little china woman on the shelf.

The little china woman had a china bonnet on her head, and china curls hung against her china neck. Her china dress was laced across in front, and she wore a pale pink china apron and little gilt china shoes. She was beautiful, standing on the shelf with flowers and leaves and birds and moons carved all around her, and the large star at the very top.

Ma was busy all day long, cooking good things for Christmas. She baked salt-rising bread and rye'n'Injun bread, and Swedish crackers, and a huge pan of baked beans, with salt pork and molasses. She baked vinegar pies and dried-

apple pies, and filled a big jar with cookies, and she let Laura and Mary lick the cake spoon.

One morning she boiled molasses and sugar together until they made a thick syrup, and Pa brought in two pans of clean, white snow from outdoors. Laura and Mary each had a pan, and Pa and Ma showed them how to pour the dark syrup in little streams on to the snow.

They made circles, and curlicues, and squiggledy things, and these hardened at once and were candy. Laura and Mary might eat one piece each, but the rest was saved for Christmas Day.

All this was done because Aunt Eliza and Uncle Peter and the cousins, Peter and Alice and Ella, were coming to spend Christmas.

The day before Christmas they came. Laura and Mary heard the gay ringing of sleigh bells, growing louder every moment, and then the big bobsled came out of the woods and drove up to the gate. Aunt Eliza and Uncle Peter and the cousins were in it, all covered up, under blankets and robes and buffalo skins.

They were wrapped up in so many coats and mufflers and veils and shawls that they looked like big, shapeless bundles.

When they all came in, the little house was full and running over. Black Susan ran out and hid in the barn, but Jack leaped in circles through the snow, barking as though he would never stop. Now there were cousins to play with!

As soon as Aunt Eliza had unwrapped them, Peter and Alice and Ella and Laura and Mary began to run and shout. At last Aunt Eliza told them to be quiet. Then Alice said:

'I'll tell you what let's do. Let's make pictures.'

Alice said they must go outdoors to do it, and Ma thought it was too cold for Laura to play outdoors. But when she saw how disappointed Laura was, she said she might go, after all, for a little while. She put on Laura's coat and mittens and the warm cape with the hood, and wrapped a muffler around her neck, and let her go.

Laura had never had so much fun. All morning she played outdoors in the snow with Alice and Ella and Peter and Mary, making pictures. The way they did it was this:

Each one by herself climbed up on a stump, and then all at once, holding their arms out wide, they fell off the stumps into the soft, deep snow. They fell flat on their faces. Then they tried to get up without spoiling the marks they made when they fell. If they did it well, there in the snow were five holes, shaped almost exactly like four little girls and a boy, arms and legs and all. They called these their pictures.

They played so hard all day that when night came they were too excited to sleep. But they must sleep, or Santa Claus would not come. So they hung their stockings by the fireplace, and said their prayers, and went to bed – Alice and Ella and Mary and Laura all in one big bed on the floor.

CHRISTMAS IS COMING

Traditional

Christmas is coming,
The geese are getting fat,
Please to put a penny
In an old man's hat;
If you haven't a penny,
A ha'penny will do,
If you haven't got a ha'penny,
God bless you!

BOY AT THE WINDOW

Extract from *Advice to a Prophet*
Richard Wilbur

Seeing the snowman standing all alone
In dusk and cold is more than he can bear.
The small boy weeps to hear the wind prepare
A night of gnashings and enormous moan.
His tearful sight can hardly reach to where
The pale-faced figure with bitumen eyes
Returns him such a god-forsaken stare
As outcast Adam gave to Paradise.

The man of snow is, nonetheless, content,
Having no wish to go inside and die.
Still, he is moved to see the youngster cry.
Though frozen water is his element,
He melts enough to drop from one soft eye
A trickle of the purest rain, a tear
For the child at the bright pane surrounded by
Such warmth, such light, such love, and so much fear.

THE SNOW MAN

Hans Christian Andersen

'It's so beautifully cold that my whole body crackles!' said the Snow Man. 'This is a kind of wind that can blow life into one, and how the gleaming one up yonder is staring at me.' He meant the sun, which was just about to set. 'It shall not make me wink – I shall manage to keep the pieces.'

He had two triangular pieces of tile in his head instead of eyes. His mouth was made of an old rake, and consequently was furnished with teeth.

He had been born amid the joyous shouts of the boys and welcomed by the sound of sledge bells and the slashing of whips.

The sun went down, and the full moon rose, round, large, clear, and beautiful in the blue air.

'There it comes again from the other side,' said the Snow Man. He intended to say the sun is showing himself again. 'Ah! I have cured him of staring. Now let him hang up there and shine, that I may see myself. If I only knew how I could manage to move from this place, I should like so much to move. If I could, I would slide along yonder on the ice, just as I see the boys slide; but I don't know how to run.'

'Off! Off!' barked the old Yard Dog. He was somewhat hoarse. He had got the hoarseness from the time when he was an indoor dog, and lay by the fire. 'The sun will teach you to run! I saw that last winter in your predecessor, and before that in his predecessor. Off! Off! – and they all go.'

'I don't understand you, comrade,' said the Snow Man. 'That thing up yonder is to teach me to run?' He meant the moon. 'Yes, it was running itself, when I looked hard at it a little while ago, and now it comes creeping from the other side.'

'You know nothing at all,' retorted the Yard Dog. 'But then you've only just been patched up. What you see yonder is the moon, and the one that went before was the sun. It will come again to-morrow, and will teach you to run down into the ditch by the wall. We shall soon have a change of weather; I can feel that in my left hind leg, for it pricks and pains me: the weather is going to change.'

'I don't understand him,' said the Snow Man; 'but I have a feeling that he's talking about something disagreeable. The one who stared so just now, and whom he called the sun, is now my friend. I can feel that.'

'Off! Off!' barked the Yard Dog; and he turned round three times, and then crept into his kennel to sleep.

The weather really changed. Towards morning, a thick damp fog lay over the whole region; later there came a wind, an icy wind. The cold seemed quite to seize upon one: but when the sun rose, what splendour! Trees and bushes were covered with hoar-frost, and looked like a complete forest of coral, and every twig seemed covered with gleaming white buds. The many delicate ramifications, concealed in summer by the wreath of leaves, now made their appearance: it seemed like a lacework, gleaming white. A snowy radiance sprang from every twig. The birch waved in the wind – it had life, like the trees in summer. It was wonderfully beautiful. And when the sun shone, how it all gleamed and sparkled, as if diamond dust had been strewn everywhere, and big diamonds had been dropped on the snowy carpet of the earth! or one could imagine that countless little lights were gleaming, whiter than even the snow itself.

'That is wonderfully beautiful,' said a young girl, who came with a young man into the garden. They both stood still near the Snow Man, and contemplated the glittering trees. 'Summer cannot show a more beautiful sight,' said she; and her eyes sparkled.

'And we can't have such a fellow as this in summer-time,' replied the young man, and he pointed to the Snow Man. 'He is capital.'

The girl laughed, nodded at the Snow Man, and then danced away over the snow with her friend – over the snow that cracked and crackled under her tread as if she were walking on starch.

'Who were those two?' the Snow Man inquired of the Yard Dog. 'You've been longer in the yard than I. Do you know them?'

'Of course I know them,' replied the Yard Dog. 'She has stroked me, and he has thrown me a meat bone. I don't bite those two.'

'But what are they?' asked the Snow Man.

'Lovers!' replied the Yard Dog. 'They will go to live in the same kennel, and gnaw at the same bone. Off! Off!'

'Are they of as much consequence as you and I?' asked the Snow Man.

'Why, they belong to the master,' retorted the Yard Dog. 'People certainly know very little who were only born yesterday. I can see that in you. I have age and information. I know everyone here in the house, and I know a time when I did not lie out here in the cold, fastened to a chain. Off! Off!'

'The cold is charming,' said the Snow Man. 'Tell me, tell me. – But you must not clank with your chain, for it jars within me when you do that.'

'Off! Off!' barked the Yard Dog. 'They told me I was a pretty little fellow: then I used to lie in a chair covered with velvet, up in master's house, and sit in the lap of the mistress of all. They used to kiss my nose, and wipe my paws with an embroidered handkerchief. I was called "Ami – dear Ami – sweet Ami". But afterwards I grew too big for them, and they gave me away to the housekeeper. So I came to live in basement story. You can look into that from where you are standing, and you can see into the room where I was master; for

I was master at the housekeeper's. It was certainly a smaller place than upstairs, but I was more comfortable, and was not continually taken hold of and pulled about by children as I had been. I received just as good food as ever, and much more. I had my own cushion, and there was a stove, the finest thing in the world at this season. I went under the stove, and could lie down quite beneath it. Ah! I still dream of that stove. Off! Off!'

'Does a stove look so beautiful?' asked the Snow Man. 'Is it at all like me?'

'It's just the reverse of you. It's as black as a crow, and has a long neck and a brazen drum. It eats firewood, so that fire spurts out of its mouth. One must keep at its side, or under it, and there one is very comfortable. You can see it through the window from where you stand.'

And the Snow Man looked and saw a bright polished thing with a brazen drum, and the fire gleamed from the lower part of it. The Snow Man felt quite strangely: an odd emotion came over him, he knew not what it meant, and could not account for it; but all people who are not snow men know the feeling.

'And why did you leave her?' asked the Snow Man, for it seemed to him that the stove must be of the female sex. 'How could you quit such a comfortable place?'

'I was obliged,' replied the Yard Dog. 'They turned me out of doors, and chained me up here. I had bitten the youngest young master in the leg, because he kicked away the bone I was gnawing. "Bone for bone," I thought. They took that very much amiss, and from that time I have been fastened to a chain and have lost my voice. Don't you hear how hoarse I am? Off! Off! that was the end of the affair.'

But the Snow Man was no longer listening to him. He was looking in at the housekeeper's basement lodgings into the room where the stove stood on its four iron legs just the same size as the Snow Man himself.

'What a strange crackling within me!' he said. 'Shall I ever get in there? It is an innocent wish, and our innocent wishes are certain to be fulfilled. It is my highest wish, my only wish, and it would be almost an injustice if it were not satisfied. I must go in there and lean against her even if I have to break through the window.'

'You will never get in there,' said the Yard Dog; 'and if you approach the stove then you are off! off!'

'I am as good as gone,' replied the Snow Man. 'I think I am breaking up.'

The whole day the Snow Man stood looking in through the window. In the twilight hour the room became still more inviting: from the stove came a mild gleam, not like the sun nor like the moon; no, it was only as the stove can glow when he has something to eat. When the room door opened, the flame started out of his mouth; this was a habit the stove had. The flame fell distinctly on the white face of the Snow Man, and gleamed red upon his bosom.

'I can endure it no longer,' said he; 'how beautiful it looks when it stretches out its tongue!'

The night was long; but it did not appear long to the Snow Man, who stood there lost in his own charming reflections, crackling with the cold.

In the morning the window-panes of the basement lodging were covered with ice. They bore the most beautiful ice-flowers that any snow man could desire; but they concealed the stove. The window-panes would not thaw; he could not see her. It crackled and whistled in him and around him; it was just the kind of frosty weather a snow man must thoroughly enjoy. But he did not

enjoy it; and, indeed, how could he enjoy himself when he was stove-sick?

'That's a terrible disease for a Snow Man,' said the Yard Dog. 'I have suffered from it myself, but I got over it. Off! Off!' he barked; and he added, 'the weather is going to change.'

And the weather did change; it began to thaw.

The warmth increased, and the Snow Man decreased. He said nothing and made no complaint – and that's an infallible sign.

One morning he broke down. And, behold, where he had stood, something like a broomstick remained sticking up out of the ground. It was the pole round which the boys had built him up.

'Ah! now I can understand why he had such an intense longing,' said the Yard Dog. 'The Snow Man has had a stove-rake in his body, and that's what moved within him. Now he has got over that too. Off! Off!'

And soon they had got over the winter.

'Off! Off!' barked the Yard Dog; but the little girls in the house sang:

'Spring out, green woodruff, fresh and fair;
Thy woolly gloves, O willow, bear.
Come, lark and cuckoo, come and sing,
Already now we greet the Spring.
I sing as well: twit-twit! cuckoo!
Come, darling Sun, and greet us too.'

And nobody thought any more of the Snow Man.

CAROLS IN GLOUCESTERSHIRE

Extract from *Cider with Rosie*
Laurie Lee

Later, towards Christmas, there was heavy snow, which raised the roads to the top of the hedges. There were millions of tons of the lovely stuff, plastic, pure, all-purpose, which nobody owned, which one could carve or tunnel, eat, or just throw about. It covered the hills and cut off the villages, but nobody thought of rescues; for there was hay in the barns and flour in the kitchens, the women baked bread, the cattle were fed and sheltered – we'd been cut off before, after all.

The week before Christmas, when snow seemed to lie thickest, was the moment for carol-singing; and when I think back to those nights it is to the crunch of snow and to the lights of the lanterns on it. Carol-singing in my village was a special tithe for the boys, the girls had little to do with it. Like hay-making, black-berrying, stone-clearing and wishing-people-a-happy-Easter, it was one of our seasonal perks.

By instinct we knew just when to begin it; a day too soon and we should have been unwelcome, a day too late and we should have received lean looks from people whose bounty was already exhausted. When the true moment came, exactly balanced, we recognized it and were ready.

So as soon as the wood had been stacked in the oven to dry for the morning fire, we put on our scarves and went out through the streets, calling loudly between our hands, till the various boys who knew the signal ran out from their houses to join us.

One by one they came stumbling over the snow, swinging their lanterns around their heads, shouting and coughing horribly.

'Coming carol-barking then?'

We were the Church Choir, so no answer was necessary. For a year we had praised the Lord out of key, and as a reward for this service – on top of the Outing – we now had the right to visit all the big houses, to sing our carols and collect our tribute.

To work them all in meant a five-mile foot journey over wild and generally snowed-up country. So the first thing we did was to plan our route; a formality, as the route never changed. All the same, we blew on our fingers and argued; and then we chose our Leader. This was not binding, for we all fancied ourselves as Leaders, and he who started the night in that position usually trailed home with a bloody nose.

Eight of us set out that night. There was Sixpence the Tanner, who had never sung in his life (he just worked his mouth in Church); the brothers Horace and Boney, who were always fighting everybody and always getting the worst of it; Clergy Green, the preaching maniac; Walt the bully, and my two brothers. As we went down the lane other boys, from other villages, were already about the hills, bawling 'Kingwenslush', and shouting through keyholes 'Knock on the knocker! Ring at the Bell! Give us a penny for singing so well!' They weren't an approved charity as we were, the Choir; but competition was in the air.

Our first call as usual was the house of the Squire, and we trouped nervously down his drive. For light we had candles in marmalade-jars suspended on loops of string, and they threw pale gleams on the towering snowdrifts that stood on each side of the drive. A blizzard was blowing, but we were well wrapped up,

with Army puttees on our legs, woollen hats on our heads, and several scarves around our ears.

As we approached the Big House across its white silent lawns, we too grew respectfully silent. The lake near by was stiff and black, the waterfall frozen and still. We arranged ourselves shuffling around the big front door, then knocked and announced the Choir.

A maid bore the tidings of our arrival away into the echoing distances of the house, and while we waited we cleared our throats noisily. Then she came back, and the door was left ajar for us, and we were bidden to begin. We brought no music, the carols were in our heads. 'Let's give 'em "Wild Shepherds",' said Jack. We began in confusion, plunging into a wreckage of keys, of different words and tempo; but we gathered our strength; he who sang loudest took the rest of us with him, and the carol took shape if not sweetness.

This huge stone house, with its ivied walls, was always a mystery to us. What were those gables, those rooms and attics, those narrow windows veiled by the cedar trees? As we sang 'Wild Shepherds' we craned our necks, gaping into that lamplit hall which we had never entered; staring at the muskets and untenanted chairs, the great tapestries furred by dust – until suddenly, on the stairs, we saw the old Squire himself standing and listening with his head on one side.

He didn't move until we'd finished; then slowly he tottered towards us, dropped two coins in our box with a trembling hand, scratched his name in the book we carried, gave us each a long look with his moist blind eyes, then turned away in silence.

As though released from a spell, we took a few sedate steps, then broke into a run for the gate. We didn't stop till we were out of the grounds. Impatient, at last, to discover the extent of his bounty, we squatted by the cowsheds, held our lanterns over the book, and saw that he had written 'Two Shillings'. This was quite a good start. No one of any worth in the district would dare to give us less than the Squire.

So with money in the box, we pushed on up the valley, pouring scorn on each other's performance. Confident now, we began to consider our quality and whether one carol was not better suited to us than another. Horace, Walt said, shouldn't sing at all; his voice was beginning to break. Horace disputed this and there was a brief token battle – they fought as they walked, kicking up divots of snow, then they forgot it, and Horace still sang.

Steadily we worked through the length of the valley, going from house to house, visiting the lesser and the greater gentry – the farmers, the doctors, the merchants, the majors and other exalted persons. It was freezing hard and blowing too; yet not for a moment did we feel the cold. The snow blew into our faces, into our eyes and mouths, soaked through our puttees, got into our boots, and dripped from our woollen caps. But we did not care. The collecting-box grew heavier, and the list of names in the book longer and more extravagant, each trying to outdo the other.

Mile after mile we went, fighting against the wind, falling into snowdrifts, and navigating by the lights of the houses. And yet we never saw our audience. We called at house after house; we sang in courtyards and porches, outside windows, or in the damp gloom of hallways; we heard voices from hidden rooms; we smelt rich clothes and strange hot food; we saw maids bearing in dishes or carrying away coffee-cups; we received nuts, cakes, figs, preserved ginger, dates, cough-drops and money; but we never once saw our patrons. We sang as it were at the castle walls, and apart from the Squire, who had shown himself to prove that he was still alive, we never expected it otherwise.

As the night drew on there was trouble with Boney. 'Noël', for instance, had a rousing harmony which Boney persisted in singing, and singing flat. The others forbade him to sing it at all, and Boney said he would fight us. Picking himself up, he agreed we were right, then he disappeared altogether. He just turned away and walked into the snow and wouldn't answer when we called him back. Much later, as we reached a far point up the valley, somebody said 'Hark!' and we stopped to listen. Far away across the fields from the distant villages came the sound of a frail voice singing, singing 'Noël', and singing it flat – it was Boney, branching out on his own.

We approached our last house high up on the hill, the place of Joseph the farmer. For him we had chosen a special carol, which was about the other Joseph, so that we always felt that singing it added a spicy cheek to the night. The last stretch of country to reach his farm was perhaps the most difficult of all. In these rough bare lanes, open to all winds, sheep were buried and wagons lost. Huddled together, we tramped in one another's footsteps, powdered snow blew into our screwed-up eyes, the candles burnt low, some blew out altogether, and we talked loudly above the gale.

Crossing, at last, the frozen mill-stream – whose wheel in summer still turned a barren mechanism – we climbed up to Joseph's farm. Sheltered by trees, warm on its bed of snow, it seemed always to be like this. As always it was late; as always this was our final call. The snow had a fine crust upon it, and the old trees sparkled like tinsel.

We grouped ourselves round the farmhouse porch. The sky cleared, and broad streams of stars ran down over the valley and away to Wales. On Slad's white slopes, seen through the black sticks of its woods, some red lamps still burned in the windows.

Everything was quiet; everywhere there was the faint crackling silence of the winter night. We started singing, and we were all moved by the words and the sudden trueness of our voices. Pure, very clear, and breathless we sang:

As Joseph was a-walking
He heard an angel sing;
'This night shall be the birth-time
Of Christ the Heavenly King.

He neither shall be bornèd
In Housen nor in hall,
Nor in a place of paradise
But in an ox's stall...'

And 2,000 Christmasses became real to us then; the houses, the halls, the places of paradise had all been visited; the stars were bright to guide the Kings through the snow; and across the farmyard we could hear the beasts in their stalls. We were given roast apples and hot mince-pies, in our nostrils were spices like myrrh, and in our wooden box, as we headed back for the village, there were golden gifts for all.

THE DECORATED FOREST

Michael Foreman

Every year, the morning before Christmas, the woodcutters came to cut down the tallest, straightest tree in the forest. The tree was taken to the village square and an old man would arrive bringing stars and streamers and all kinds of decorations from his workshop in the mountains.

This year, as usual, the woodcutters had cut down the tallest, straightest tree and set it up in the square. The children waited for the decorations. But the old man did not arrive.

He had set off from the snowy peaks, but near the centre of the forest he had sat down for a rest. There he listened to the birds arguing and complaining to an old owl.

The owl, in a very bent and twisted tree, was shrugging his shoulders and shaking his head, saying 'I told you soo, I told you soo...'

'But we have nowhere to live,' cried the birds.

'They've chopped down our tree.'

'Of course,' said the owl. 'I told you not to live in the tallest, straightest tree, but you wouldn't listen. You thought you would be higher than everyone else and you always laughed at my home. However, you are welcome to stay with me over Christmas.'

The old man was moved by the kindness and wisdom of the old owl and
wanted to make Christmas in the old tree a success. He chose a few of the most
beautiful stars from his sack and began to decorate the branches. The owl was
delighted and the other birds sang approval as each new star was added.

Meanwhile, the children in the village were still waiting. They waited all morning and most of the afternoon.

At last, they set out to look for the old man. But they did not come back. Later, a search party was sent to look for the children, and finally the whole village went in search of the search party.

They found the search party and the children and the old man and all the animals and birds dancing in the light of the moon. In the middle stood the most beautiful tree they had ever seen. The villagers hesitated for a moment and then, they too, joined in the dance. Food was brought at midnight and they sang carols all the way home.

That Christmas Day, and every Christmas after, was celebrated in the forest. The old man made more decorations than ever, and every tree had a star and they never needed to chop down the tallest, straightest tree ever again.

THE TASK

Extract
William Cowper

Forth goes the woodman, leaving unconcern'd
The cheerful haunts of man; to wield the axe
And drive the wedge, in younder forest drear
From morn to eve his solitary task.
Shaggy, and lean, and shrewd, with pointed ears
And tail cropp'd short, half lurcher and half cur –
His dog attends him. Close behind his heel
Now creeps he slow; and now, with many a frisk
Wide-scamp'ring, snatches up the drifted snow
With iv'ry teeth, or ploughs it with his snout;
Then shakes his powder'd coat, and barks for joy.
Heedless of all his pranks, the sturdy churl
Moves right toward the mark; nor stops for aught,
But now and then with pressure of his thumb
T'adjust the fragrant charge of a short tube
That fumes beneath his nose: the trailing cloud
Streams far behind him, scenting all the air...

WINTER MORNING

Ogden Nash

Winter is the king of showmen,
Turning tree stumps into snow men
And houses into birthday cakes
And spreading sugar over the lakes.
Smooth and clean and frost white
The world looks good enough to bite.
That's the season to be young,
Catching snowflakes on your tongue.

Snow is snowy when it's snowing
I'm sorry it's slushy when it's going.

THE GIFT OF THE MAGI

O. Henry

One dollar and eighty-seven cents. That was all. And sixty cents of it was in pennies. Pennies saved one and two at a time by bulldozing the grocer and the vegetable man and the butcher until one's cheeks burned with the silent imputation of parsimony that such close dealing implied. Three times Della counted it. One dollar and eighty-seven cents. And the next day would be Christmas.

There was clearly nothing to do but flop down on the shabby little couch and howl. So Della did it. Which instigates the moral reflection that life is made up of sobs, sniffles, and smiles, with sniffles predominating.

While the mistress of the home is gradually subsiding from the first stage to the second, take a look at the home. A furnished flat at $8 per week. It did not exactly beggar description, but it certainly had that word on the lookout for the mendicancy squad.

In the vestibule below was a letter-box into which no letter would go, and an electric button from which no mortal finger could coax a ring. Also appertaining thereunto was a card bearing the name 'Mr James Dillingham Young'.

The 'Dillingham' had been flung to the breeze during a former period of prosperity when its possessor was being paid $30 per week. Now, when the income was shrunk to $20, the letters of 'Dillingham' looked blurred, as though they were thinking seriously of contracting to a modest and unassuming D. But whenever Mr James Dillingham Young came home and reached his flat above he was called 'Jim' and greatly hugged by Mrs James Dillingham Young, already introduced to you as Della. Which is all very good.

Della finished her cry and attended to her cheeks with the powder rag. She stood by the window and looked out dully at a grey cat walking a grey fence in a grey backyard. Tomorrow would be Christmas Day, and she had only $1.87 with which to buy Jim a present. She had been saving every penny she could for months, with this result. Twenty dollars a week doesn't go far. Expenses had been greater than she had calculated. They always are. Only $1.87 to buy a present for Jim. Her Jim. Many a happy hour she had spent planning for something nice for him. Something fine and rare and sterling – something just a little bit near to being worthy of the honour of being owned by Jim.

There was a pier-glass between the windows of the room. Perhaps you have seen a pier-glass in an $8 flat. A very thin and very agile person may, by observing his reflection in a rapid sequence of longitundinal strips, obtain a fairly accurate conception of his looks. Della, being slender, had mastered the art.

Suddenly she whirled from the window and stood before the glass. Her eyes were shining brilliantly, but her face had lost its colour within twenty seconds. Rapidly she pulled down her hair and let it fall to its full length.

Now, there were two possessions of the James Dillingham Youngs in which they both took a mighty pride. One was Jim's gold watch that had been his father's and his grandfather's. The other was Della's hair. Had the Queen of Sheba lived in the flat across the airshaft, Della would have let her hair hang out the window some day to dry just to depreciate Her Majesty's jewels and gifts. Had King Solomon been the janitor, with all his treasures piled up in the basement, Jim would have pulled out his watch every time he passed, just to see him pluck at his beard from envy.

So now Della's beautiful hair fell about her rippling and shining like a cascade of brown waters. It reached below her knee and made itself almost a garment for her. And then she did it up again nervously and quickly. Once she faltered for a minute and stood still while a tear or two splashed on the worn red carpet.

On went her old brown jacket; on went her old brown hat. With a whirl of skirts and with the brilliant sparkle still in her eyes, she fluttered out the door and down the stairs to the street.

Where she stopped the sign read: 'Mme Sofronie. Hair Goods of All Kinds.'

One flight up Della ran, and collected herself, panting. Madame, large, too white, chilly, hardly looked the 'Sofronie'.

'Will you buy my hair?' asked Della.

'I buy hair,' said Madame. 'Take yer hat off and let's have a sight at the looks of it.'

Down rippled the brown cascade.

'Twenty dollars,' said Madame, lifting the mass with a practised hand.

'Give it to me quick,' said Della.

Oh, and the next two hours tripped by on rosy wings. Forget the hashed metaphor. She was ransacking the stores for Jim's present.

She found it at last. It surely had been made for Jim and no one else. There was no other like it in any of the stores, and she had turned all of them inside out. It was a platinum fob chain simple and chaste in design, properly proclaiming its value by substance alone and not by meretricious ornamentation – as all good things should do. It was even worthy of The Watch. As soon as she saw it she knew that it must be Jim's. It was like him. Quietness and value – the description applied to both. Twenty-one dollars they took from her for it, and she hurried home with the 87 cents. With that chain on his watch Jim might be properly anxious about the time in any company. Grand as the watch was, he sometimes looked at it on the sly on account of the old leather strap that he used in place of a chain.

When Della reached home her intoxication gave way a little to prudence and reason. She got out her curling irons and lighted the gas and went to work repairing the ravages made by generosity added to love. Which is always a tremendous task, dear friends – a mammoth task.

Within forty minutes her head was covered with tiny, close-lying curls that made her look wonderfully like a truant schoolboy. She looked at her reflection in the mirror long, carefully, and critically.

'If Jim doesn't kill me,' she said to herself, 'before he takes a second look at me, he'll say I look like a Coney Island chorus girl. But what could I do – oh!

what could I do with a dollar and eighty-seven cents?'

At 7 o'clock the coffee was made and the frying-pan was on the back of the stove hot and ready to cook the chops.

Jim was never late. Della doubled the fob chain in her hand and sat on the corner of the table near the door that he always entered. Then she heard his step on the stair away down on the first flight, and she turned white for just a moment. She had a habit of saying little silent prayers about the simplest everyday things, and now she whispered: 'Please God, make him think I am still pretty.'

The door opened and Jim stepped in and closed it. He looked thin and very serious. Poor fellow, he was only twenty-two – and to be burdened with a family! He needed a new overcoat and he was without gloves.

Jim stopped inside the door, as immovable as a setter at the scent of quail. His eyes were fixed upon Della, and there was an expression in them that she could not read, and it terrified her. It was not anger, nor surprise, nor disapproval, nor horror, nor any of the sentiments that she had been prepared for. He simply stared at her fixedly with that peculiar expression on his face.

Della wriggled off the table and went for him.

'Jim, darling,' she cried, 'don't look at me that way. I had my hair cut off and sold it because I couldn't have lived through Christmas without giving you a present. It'll grow out again – you won't mind, will you? I just had to do it. My hair grows awfully fast. Say "Merry Christmas!" Jim, and let's be happy. You don't know what a nice – what a beautiful, nice gift I've got for you.'

'You've cut off your hair?' asked Jim, laboriously, as if he had not arrived at that patent fact yet even after the hardest mental labour.

'Cut it off and sold it,' said Della. 'Don't you like me just as well, anyhow? I'm me without my hair, ain't I?'

Jim looked about the room curiously.

'You say your hair is gone?' he said, with an air almost of idiocy.

'You needn't look for it,' said Della. 'It's sold, I tell you – sold and gone, too. It's Christmas Eve, boy. Be good to me, for it went for you. Maybe the hairs of my head were numbered,' she went on with a sudden sweetness, 'but nobody could ever count my love for you. Shall I put the chops on, Jim?'

Out of his trance Jim seemed quickly to wake. He enfolded his Della. For ten seconds let us regard with discreet scrutiny some inconsequential object in the other direction. Eight dollars a week or a million a year – what is the difference? A mathematician or a wit would give you the wrong answer. The magi brought valuable gifts, but that was not among them. This dark assertion will be illuminated later on.

Jim drew a package from his overcoat pocket and threw it upon the table.

'Don't make any mistake, Dell,' he said, 'about me. I don't think there's anything in the way of a haircut or a shave or a shampoo that could make me like my girl any less. But if you'll unwrap that package you may see why you had me going a while at first.'

White fingers and nimble tore at the string and paper. And then an ecstatic scream of joy; and then, alas! a quick feminine change to hysterical tears and wails, necessitating the immediate employment of all the comforting powers of the lord of the flat.

For there lay The Combs – the set of combs, side and back, that Della had worshipped for long in a Broadway window. Beautiful combs, pure tortoise

shell, with jewelled rims – just the shade to wear in the beautiful vanished hair. They were expensive combs, she knew, and her heart had simply craved and yearned over them without the least hope of possession. And now, they were hers, but the tresses that should have adorned the coveted adornments were gone.

But she hugged them to her bosom, and at length she was able to look up with dim eyes and a smile and say: 'My hair grows so fast, Jim!'

And then Della leaped up like a little singed cat and cried, 'Oh, oh!'

Jim had not yet seen his beautiful present. She held it out to him eagerly upon her open palm. The dull precious metal seemed to flash with a reflection of her bright and ardent spirit.

'Isn't it a dandy, Jim? I hunted all over town to find it. You'll have to look at the time a hundred times a day now. Give me your watch. I want to see how it looks on it.'

Instead of obeying, Jim tumbled down on the couch and put his hands under the back of his head and smiled.

'Dell,' said he, 'let's put our Christmas presents away and keep 'em a while. They're too nice to use just at present. I sold the watch to get the money to buy your combs. And now suppose you put the chops on.'

The magi, as you know, were wise men – wonderfully wise men – who brought gifts to the Babe in the manger. They invented the art of giving Christmas presents. Being wise, their gifts were no doubt wise ones, possibly bearing the privilege of exchange in case of duplication. And here I have lamely related to you the uneventful chronicle of two foolish children in a flat who most unwisely sacrificed for each other the greatest treasures of their house. But in a last word to the wise of these days let it be said that of all who give gifts these two were the wisest. Of all who give and receive gifts, such as they are wisest. Everywhere they are wisest. They are the magi.

THE CHRISTMAS STORY

Extract from *The King James Bible*

In the days of Herod the King, the angel Gabriel was sent from God unto a city named Nazareth, to a virgin espoused to a man whose name was Joseph; and the virgin's name was Mary.

And the angel said, Thou shalt bring forth a son, and shalt call his name Jesus. He shall be called the Son of the Highest: and of his kingdom there shall be no end.

And Mary said, Behold the handmaid of the Lord. And the angel departed from her.

It came to pass that there went out a decree that all the world should be taxed, every one in his own city. And Joseph went up from Nazareth to the city called Bethlehem, to be taxed with Mary his wife, being great with child.

And she brought forth her firstborn son, and wrapped him in swaddling clothes, and laid him in a manger; because there was no room for them in the inn.

There were in the same country shepherds keeping watch over their flock by night. And the angel of the Lord came upon them, and they were sore afraid.

And the angel said unto them, Fear not: for behold, I bring you good tidings of great joy. For unto you is born a Saviour, which is Christ the Lord. And this shall be a sign unto you; ye shall find the babe wrapped in swaddling clothes, lying in a manger.

Suddenly there was a multitude of the heavenly host saying, Glory to God in the highest, and on earth peace, good will toward men.

The shepherds said one to another, Let us now go to Bethlehem. And they found Mary and Joseph, and the babe lying in a manger.

And all they that heard it wondered at those things which were told them by the shepherds. But Mary kept all these things, and pondered them in her heart.

And the shepherds returned, praising God.

Behold, there came wise men from the east, saying, Where is he that is born King of the Jews? For we have seen his star in the east, and are come to worship him.

When Herod the King heard these things, he was troubled. And he sent them to Bethlehem, and said, Go and search diligently for the child; and when ye have found him, bring me word again, that I may come and worship him also.

When they had heard the King, they departed; and lo, the star went before them, till it stood over where the young child was.

And they saw the young child with Mary his mother, and fell down and worshipped him; and when they had opened their treasures, they presented unto him gifts: gold, and frankincense, and myrrh.

Being warned in a dream that they should not return to Herod, they departed into their own country another way.

And the angel appeared to Joseph in a dream, saying, Arise, and take the child and his mother, and flee into Egypt, for Herod will seek the child to destroy him.

When he arose, he took the child and his mother by night, and departed into Egypt, and was there until the death of Herod.

But when Herod was dead, an angel appeared in a dream to Joseph in Egypt, saying, Take the child and his mother, and go into the land of Israel: for they are dead which sought the young child's life.

And he took the child and his mother and came into the land of Israel, and dwelt in Nazareth.

And the child grew, and waxed strong in spirit, filled with wisdom: and the grace of God was upon him.

THE OXEN

Thomas Hardy

Christmas Eve, and twelve of the clock.
'Now they are all on their knees,'
An elder said as we sat in a flock
By the embers in hearthside ease.

We pictured the meek mild creatures where
They dwelt in their strawy pen,
Nor did it occur to one of us there
To doubt they were kneeling then.

So fair a fancy few would weave
In these years! Yet, I feel,
If someone said on Christmas Eve,
'Come; see the oxen kneel

'In the lonely barton by yonder coomb
Our childhood used to know,'
I should go with him in the gloom,
Hoping it might be so.

A Christmas Carol

G. K. Chesterton

The Christ-child lay on Mary's lap,
His hair was like a light,
(O weary, weary were the world,
But here is all aright.)

The Christ-child lay on Mary's breast,
His hair was like a star.
(O stern and cunning are the kings,
But here the true hearts are.)

The Christ-child lay on Mary's heart,
His hair was like a fire.
(O weary, weary is the world,
But here the world's desire.)

The Christ-child stood at Mary's knee,
His hair was like a crown,
And all the flowers looked up at him,
And all the stars looked down.

Stopping by Woods on a Snowy Evening

Robert Frost

Whose woods these are I think I know.
His house is in the village, though;
He will not see me stopping here
To watch his woods fill up with snow.

My little horse must think it queer
To stop without a farmhouse near
Between the woods and frozen lake
The darkest evening of the year.

He gives his harness bells a shake
To ask if there is some mistake.
The only other sound's the sweep
Of easy wind and downy flake.

The woods are lovely, dark, and deep,
But I have promises to keep,
And miles to go before I sleep,
And miles to go before I sleep.

THE NIGHT
BEFORE CHRISTMAS

Clement C. Moore

'Twas the night before Christmas, when all through the house
Not a creature was stirring, not even a mouse;
The stockings were hung by the chimney with care,
In hopes that St. Nicholas soon would be there.
The children were nestled all snug in their beds,
While visions of sugarplums danced in their heads;
And Mama in her kerchief and I in my cap,
Had just settled down for a long winter's nap –
When out on the lawn there rose such a clatter,
I sprang from my bed to see what was the matter.
Away to the window I flew like a flash,
Tore open the shutters and threw up the sash.

The moon on the breast of the new-fallen snow,

Gave a luster of midday to objects below;

When, what to my wondering eyes should appear,

But a miniature sleigh and eight tiny reindeer,

With a little old driver so lively and quick,

I knew in a moment it must be St. Nick.

More rapid than eagles his coursers they came,

And he whistled, and shouted, and called them by name –

'Now, Dasher! Now, Dancer! Now, Prancer and Vixen!

On, Comet! On, Cupid! On, Donder and Blitzen!

To the top of the porch, to the top of the wall!

Now, dash away! Dash away! Dash away all!'

As dry leaves before the wild hurricane fly,

When they meet with an obstacle, mount to the sky,

So up to the housetop the coursers they flew,

With sleigh full of toys – and St. Nicholas too;

And then in a twinkling, I heard on the roof

The prancing and pawing of each little hoof.

As I drew in my head and was turning around,

Down the chimney St. Nicholas came with a bound.

He was dressed all in fur from his head to his foot,

And his clothes were all tarnished with ashes and soot.

A bundle of toys he had flung on his back,

And he looked like a peddler just opening his pack.

His eyes how they twinkled! His dimples how merry!
His cheeks were like roses, his nose like a cherry!
His droll little mouth was drawn up like a bow,
And the beard on his chin was as white as the snow!
The stump of a pipe he held tight in his teeth,
And the smoke it encircled his head like a wreath.
He had a broad face and a little round belly
That shook when he laughed like a bowl full of jelly.
He was chubby and plump – a right jolly old elf,
And I laughed when I saw him, in spite of myself.
A wink of his eye and a twist of his head,
Soon gave me to know I had nothing to dread.

He spoke not a word, but went straight to his work,
And filled all the stockings then turned with a jerk.
And laying his finger aside of his nose,
And giving a nod, up the chimney he rose.
He sprang to his sleigh, to his team gave a whistle,
And away they all flew like the down of a thistle.
But I heard him exclaim as he drove out of sight,
'Merry Christmas to all and to all a Good Night!'

N<small>O</small> M<small>AN'S</small> L<small>AND</small>

Extract from *War Game*
Michael Foreman

The weather, still wet, grew steadily cooler. Then, one night, as the lads returned to the Front after a few days' rest, the rain stopped and it grew bitterly cold.

That night they were relieving a Scottish regiment, and as the Scots left the Line, the Germans shouted Christmas wishes to them.

Then tiny lights appeared in the German trenches. As far as the eye could see, Christmas trees were flickering along the parapet of the German lines.

It was Christmas Eve.

A single German voice began to sing 'Silent Night'. It was joined by many others.

The British replied with 'The First Noel' to applause from the Germans. And so it went on, turn and turn about. Then both front lines sang 'O Come All Ye Faithful'.

It was a beautiful moonlit night. Occasionally a star shell hung like a Star of Bethlehem.

At dawn, when the British were all 'Stood To' on the fire-step, they saw a world white with frost. The few shattered trees that remained were white. Lines of wire glinted like tinsel. The humps of dead in No Man's Land were like toppled snowmen.

After the singing of the night, the Christmas dawn was strangely quiet. The clock of death had stopped ticking.

Then a German climbed from his trench and planted a Christmas tree in No Man's Land. Freddie, being a goalkeeper and therefore a bit daft, walked out and shook hands with him. Both sides applauded.

A small group of men from each side, unarmed, joined them. They all shook hands. One of the Germans spoke good English and said he hoped the war would end soon because he wanted to return to his job as a taxi driver in Birmingham.

It was agreed that they should take the opportunity to bury the dead. The bodies were mixed up together. They were sorted out, and a joint burial service was held on the 'halfway line'.

Both sides then returned to their trenches for breakfast. Will and the lads were cheered by the wonderful smell of bacon, and they had a hot breakfast for a change.

One by one, birds began to arrive from all sides. The soldiers hardly ever saw a bird normally, but Will counted at least fifty sparrows hopping around their trench.

Christmas presents for the men consisted of a packet of chocolate, Oxo cubes, a khaki handkerchief, peppermints, camp cocoa, writing paper and a pencil. After breakfast a pair of horses and a wagon arrived with Princess Mary's Christmas gifts – a pipe and tobacco and a Christmas card from the King and Queen.

There were no planes overhead, no observation balloons, no bombs, no rifle fire, no snipers, just an occasional skylark. The early mist lifted to reveal a clear blue sky. The Germans were strolling about on their parapet once more, and waved to the British to join them. Soon there was quite a crowd in No Man's Land. Both sides exchanged small gifts. One German had been a barber in Holborn in London. A chair was placed on the 'halfway line' and he gave haircuts to several of the British officers.

Then from somewhere a football came across the frozen mud. Will was on it in a flash. He trapped the ball with his left foot, flipped it up with his right, and headed it towards Freddie.

Freddie made a spectacular dive, caught the ball in both hands and threw it to a group of Germans. Immediately a vast, fast and furious football match was underway. Goals were marked by caps. Freddie, of course, was in one goal and a huge German in the other.

Apart from that, it was wonderfully disorganized, part football, part ice-skating, with unknown numbers on each team. No referee, no account of the score.

I Saw Three Ships

Traditional

I saw three ships come sailing by,
On Christmas Day, on Christmas Day,
I saw three ships come sailing by,
On Christmas Day in the morning.

And who was in those ships all three,
On Christmas Day, on Christmas Day,
And who was in those ships all three,
On Christmas Day in the morning?

Our Saviour Christ and His Lady,
On Christmas Day, on Christmas Day,
Our Saviour Christ and His Lady,
On Christmas Day in the morning.

Oh! they sailed into Bethlehem,
On Christmas Day, on Christmas Day,
Oh! they sailed into Bethlehem,
On Christmas Day in the morning.

And all the bells on earth shall ring,
On Christmas Day, on Christmas Day,
And all the bells on earth shall ring,
On Christmas Day in the morning.

And all the Angels in Heaven shall sing,
On Christmas Day, on Christmas Day,
And all the Angels in Heaven shall sing,
On Christmas Day in the morning.

And all the souls on earth shall sing,
On Christmas Day, on Christmas Day,
And all the souls on earth shall sing,
On Christmas Day in the morning.

CHRISTMAS AT SEA

Robert Louis Stevenson

The sheets were frozen hard, and they cut the naked hand;
The decks were like a slide, where a seaman scarce could stand.
The wind was a nor'wester, blowing squally off the sea;
The cliffs and spouting breakers were the only things a-lee.

They heard the surf a-roaring before the break of day;
But 'twas only with the peep of light we saw how ill we lay.
We tumbled every hand on deck instanter, with a shout,
And we gave her the maintops'l, and stood by to go about.

All day we tacked and tacked between the South Head and the North;
All day we hauled the frozen sheets, and got no further forth;
All day as cold as charity, in bitter pain and dread,
For very life and nature we tacked from head to head.

We gave the South a wider berth, for there the tide-race roared;
But every tack we made we brought the North Head close aboard:
So's we saw the cliffs and houses, and the breakers running high
And the coastguard in his garden, with his glass against his eye.

The frost was on the village roofs as white as ocean foam;
The good red fires were burning bright in every 'longshore home;
The windows sparkled clear, and the chimneys volleyed out;
And I vow we sniffed the victuals as the vessel went about.

The bells upon the church were rung with a mighty jovial cheer;
For it's just that I should tell you how (of all days in the year)
This day of our adversity was blessed Christmas morn,
And the house above the coastguard's was the house where I was born.

O well I saw the pleasant room, the pleasant faces there,
My mother's silver spectacles, my father's silver hair;
And well I saw the firelight, like a flight of homely elves,
Go dancing round the china-plates that stand upon the shelves.

And well I knew the talk they had, they talk that was of me,
Of the shadow on the household and the son that went to sea;
And O the wicked fool I seemed, in every kind of way,
To be here and hauling frozen ropes on blessed Christmas Day.

They lit the high sea-light, and the dark began to fall.
'All hands to loose topgallant sails,' I heard the captain call.
'By the Lord, she'll never stand it,' our first mate, Jackson, cried.
...'It's the one way or the other, Mr Jackson,' he replied.

She staggered to her bearings, but the sails were new and good,
And the ship smelt up to windward just as though she understood.
As the winter's day was ending, in the entry of the night
We cleared the weary headland, and passed below the light.

And they heaved a mighty breath, every soul on board but me,
As they saw her nose again pointing handsome out to sea;
But all that I could think of, in the darkness and the cold,
Was just that I was leaving home and my folks were growing old.

CHRISTMAS SHOPS

Extract from *A Christmas Carol*
Charles Dickens

For the people who were shovelling away on the housetops were jovial and full of glee; calling out to one another from the parapets, and now and then exchanging a facetious snowball – better-natured missile far than many a wordy jest – laughing heartily if it went right, and not less heartily if it went wrong. The poulterers' shops were still half open, and the fruiterers' were radiant in their glory. There were great round, pot-bellied baskets of chestnuts, shaped like the waistcoats of jolly old gentlemen, lolling at the doors, and tumbling out into the street in their apoplectic opulence. There were ruddy, brown-faced, broad-girthed Spanish Onions, shining in the fatness of their growth like Spanish Friars; and winking from their shelves in wanton slyness at the girls as they went by, and glanced demurely at the hung-up mistletoe. There were pears and apples, clustered high in blooming pyramids; there were bunches of grapes, made in the shopkeepers' benevolence to dangle from conspicuous hooks, that people's mouths might water gratis as they passed; there were piles of filberts, mossy and brown, recalling, in their fragrance, ancient walks among the woods, and pleasant shufflings ankle deep through withered leaves; there were Norfolk Biffins, squab and swarthy, setting off the yellow of the oranges and lemons, and in the great compactness of their juicy persons, urgently entreating and beseeching to be carried home in paper bags and eaten after dinner. The very gold and silver fish, set forth among these choice fruits in a bowl, though members of a dull and stagnant-blooded race, appeared to know that there was something going on; and, to a fish, went gasping round and round their little world in slow and passionless excitement.

The Grocers'! oh the Grocers'! nearly closed, with perhaps two shutters down, or one; but through those gaps such glimpses! It was not alone that the scales descending on the counter made a merry sound, or that the twine and roller parted company so briskly, or that the canisters were rattled up and down like juggling tricks, or even that the blended scents of tea and coffee were so grateful to the nose, or even that the raisins were so plentiful and rare, the almonds so extremely white, the sticks of cinnamon so long and straight, the other spices so delicious, the candied fruits

so caked and spotted with molten sugar as to make the coldest lookers-on feel faint and subsequently bilious. Nor was it that the figs were moist and pulpy, or that the French plums blushed in modest tartness from their highly-decorated boxes, or that everything was good to eat and in its Christmas dress: but the customers were all so hurried and so eager in the hopeful promise of the day, that they tumbled up against each other at the door, clashing their wicker baskets wildly, and left their purchases upon the counter, and came running back to fetch them, and committed hundreds of the like mistakes in the best humour possible; while the Grocer and his people were so frank and fresh that the polished hearts with which they fastened their aprons behind might have been their own, worn outside for general inspection, and for the Christmas daws to peck at if they chose.

But soon the steeples called good people all, to church and chapel, and away they came, flocking through the streets in their best clothes, and with their gayest faces. And at the same time there emerged from scores of bye streets, lanes and nameless turnings, innumerable people, carrying their dinners to the bakers' shops.

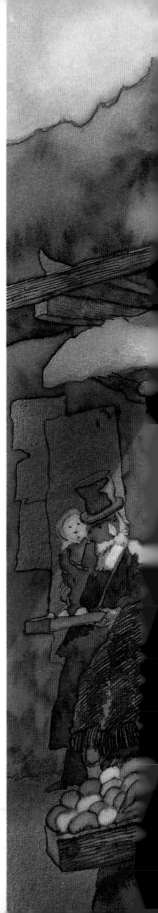

COWBOY CAROL

Cecil Broadhurst

There'll be a new world beginin' from t'night!
There'll be a new world beginin' from t'night!
When I climb up to my saddle
Gonna take Him to my heart.
There'll be a new world beginin' from t'night!

Right across the prairie,
Clear across the valley,
Straight across the heart of ev'ry man,
There'll be a right new brand of livin'
That'll sweep like lightnin' fire
And take away the hate in ev'ry land.

There'll be a new world beginin' from t'night!
There'll be a new world beginin' from t'night!
When I climb up to my saddle
Gonna take Him to my heart.
There'll be a new world beginin' from t'night!

Yay! Yippee! We're gonna ride the trail!
Yay! Yippee! We're gonna ride today!
When I climb up to my saddle
Gonna take Him to my heart!
There'll be a new world beginin' from t'night.

OUTDOOR SONG

Extract from *Winnie the Pooh*
A. A. Milne

The more it
SNOWS – tiddely-pom
The more it
GOES – tiddely-pom
The more it
GOES – tiddely-pom
On
Snowing.

And nobody
KNOWS – tiddely-pom
How cold my
TOES – tiddely-pom
How cold my
TOES – tiddely-pom
Are
Growing.

CHRISTMAS UNDERGROUND

Extract from *The Wind in the Willows*
Kenneth Grahame

'What a capital little house this is!' Mr Rat called out cheerily. 'So compact! So well planned! Everything here and everything in its place! We'll make a jolly night of it. The first thing we want is a good fire; I'll see to that – I always know where to find things. So this is the parlour? Splendid! Your own idea, those little sleeping-bunks in the wall? Capital! Now, I'll fetch the wood and the coals, and you get a duster, Mole – you'll find one in the drawer of the kitchen table – and try and smarten things up a bit. Bustle about, old chap!'

Encouraged by his inspiriting companion, the Mole roused himself and dusted and polished with energy and heartiness, while the Rat, running to and fro with armfuls of fuel, soon had a cheerful blaze roaring up the chimney. He hailed the Mole to come and warm himself; but Mole promptly had another fit of the blues, dropping down on a couch in dark despair and burying his face in his duster.

'Rat,' he moaned, 'how about your supper, you poor, cold, hungry, weary animal? I've nothing to give you – nothing – not a crumb!'

'What a fellow you are for giving in!' said the Rat reproachfully. 'Why, only just now I saw a sardine-opener on the kitchen dresser, quite distinctly; and everybody knows that means there are sardines about somewhere in the neighbourhood. Rouse yourself! pull yourself together, and come with me and forage.'

They went and foraged accordingly, hunting through every cupboard and turning out every drawer. The result was not so very depressing after all, though of course it might have been better; a tin of sardines – a box of captain's biscuits, nearly full – and a German sausage encased in silver paper.

'There's a banquet for you!' observed the Rat, as he arranged the table. 'I know some animals who would give their ears to be sitting down to supper with us tonight!'

'No bread!' groaned the Mole dolorously; 'no butter, no –'

'No *pâté de foie gras*, no champagne!' continued the Rat, grinning. 'And that reminds me – what's that little door at the end of the passage? Your cellar, of course! Every luxury in this house! Just you wait a minute.'

He made for the cellar door, and presently re-appeared, somewhat dusty, with a bottle of beer in each paw and another under each arm. 'Self-indulgent beggar you seem to be, Mole,' he observed. 'Deny yourself nothing. This is really the jolliest little place I ever was in. Now, wherever did you pick up those prints? Make the place look so home-like, they do. No wonder you're so fond of it, Mole. Tell us all about it, and how you came to make it what it is.'

Then, while the Rat busied himself fetching plates, and knives and forks, and mustard which he mixed in an egg-cup, the Mole, his bosom still heaving with the stress of his recent emotion, related – somewhat shyly at first, but with more freedom as he warmed to his subject – how this was planned, and how that was thought out, and how this was got through a windfall from an aunt, and that was a wonderful find and a bargain, and this other thing was bought out of laborious savings and a certain amount of 'going without'. His spirits finally quite restored, he must needs go and caress his possessions, and take a lamp and show off their points to his visitor, and expatiate on them, quite forgetful of the supper they both so much needed; Rat, who was desperately hungry but strove to conceal it, nodding seriously, examining with a puckered brow, and saying, 'Wonderful', and 'Most remarkable', at intervals, when the chance for an observation was given him.

At last the Rat succeeded in decoying him to the table, and had just got seriously to work with the sardine-opener when sounds were heard from the forecourt without – sounds like the scuffling of small feet in the gravel and a confused murmur of tiny voices, while broken sentences reached them – 'Now, all in a line – hold the lantern up a bit, Tommy – clear your throats first – no coughing after I say one, two, three. – Where's young Bill? – Here, come on, do, we're all a-waiting –'

'What's up?' inquired the Rat, pausing in his labours.

'I think it must be the field-mice,' replied the Mole, with a touch of pride in his manner. 'They go round carol-singing regularly at this time of the year. They're quite an institution in these parts. And they never pass me over – they come to Mole End last of all; and I used to give them hot drinks, and supper sometimes, when I could afford it. It will be like old times to hear them again.'

'Let's have a look at them!' cried the Rat, jumping up and running to the door.

It was a pretty sight, and a seasonable one, that met their eyes when they flung the door open. In the forecourt, lit by the dim rays of a horn lantern, some eight or ten little field-mice stood in a semi-circle, red worsted comforters round their throats, their forepaws thrust deep into their pockets, their feet jigging for warmth. With bright beady eyes they glanced shyly at each other, sniggering a little, sniffing and applying coat-sleeves a good deal. As the door opened, one of the elder ones that carried the lantern was just saying, 'Now then, one, two, three!' and forthwith their shrill little voices uprose on the air, singing one of the old-time carols that their forefathers composed in fields that were fallow and held by frost, or when snow-bound in chimney corners, and handed down to be sung in the miry street to lamp-lit windows at Yule-time.

Villagers all, this frosty tide,
Let your doors swing open wide,
Though wind may follow, and snow beside,
Yet draw us in by your fire to bide;
Joy shall be yours in the morning!

Here we stand in the cold and the sleet,
Blowing fingers and stamping feet,
Come from far away you to greet –
You by the fire and we in the street –
Bidding you joy in the morning!

For ere one half of the night was gone,
Sudden a star has led us on,
Raining bliss and benison –
Bliss tomorrow and more anon,
Joy for every morning!

Goodman Joseph toiled through the snow –
Saw the star o'er a stable low;
Mary she might not further go –
Welcome thatch, and litter below!
Joy was hers in the morning!

And when they heard the angels tell
'Who were the first to cry Nowell?
Animals all, as it befell,
In the stable where they did dwell!
Joy shall be theirs in the morning!'

The voices ceased, the singers, bashful but smiling, exchanged sidelong glances, and silence succeeded – but for a moment only. Then, from up above and far away, down the tunnel they had so lately travelled was borne to their ears in a faint musical hum the sound of distant bells ringing a joyful and clangorous peal.

'Very well sung, boys!' cried the Rat heartily. 'And now come along in, all of you, and warm yourselves by the fire, and have something hot!'

'Yes, come along, field-mice,' cried the Mole eagerly. 'This is quite like old times! Shut the door after you. Pull up that settle to the fire. Now, you just wait a minute, while we – O, Ratty!' he cried in despair, plumping down on a seat, with tears impending. 'Whatever are we doing? We've nothing to give them!'

'You leave all that to me,' said the masterful Rat. 'Here, you with the lantern! Come over this way. I want to talk to you.

'Now, tell me, are there any shops open at this hour of the night?'

'Why, certainly, sir,' replied the field-mouse respectfully. 'At this time of the year our shops keep open to all sorts of hours.'

'Then look here!' said the Rat. 'You go off at once, you and your lantern, and you get me –'

Here much muttered conversation ensued, and the Mole only heard bits of it, such as – 'Fresh, mind! – no, a pound of that will do – see you get Buggins's, for I won't have any other – no, only the best – if you can't get it there, try somewhere else – yes, of course, home-made, no tinned stuff – well then, do the best you can!' Finally, there was a chink of coin passing from paw to paw, the field-mouse was provided with an ample basket for his purchases, and off he hurried, he and his lantern.

The rest of the field-mice, perched in a row on the settle, their small legs swinging, gave themselves up to the enjoyment of the fire, and toasted their chillblains till they tingled; while the Mole, failing to draw them into easy conversation, plunged into family history and made each of them recite the names of his numerous brothers, who were too young, it appeared, to be allowed to go out a-carolling this year, but looked forward very shortly to winning the parental consent.

The Rat, meanwhile, was busy examining the label on one of the beer-bottles. 'I perceive this to be Old Burton,' he remarked approvingly. '*Sensible* Mole! The very thing! Now we shall be able to mull some ale! Get the things ready, Mole, while I draw the corks.'

It did not take long to prepare the brew and thrust the tin heater well into the red heart of the fire; and soon every field-mouse was sipping and coughing and choking (for a little mulled ale goes a long way) and wiping his eyes and laughing and forgetting he had ever been cold in all his life.

'They act plays too, these fellows,' the Mole explained to the Rat. 'Make them up all by themselves, and act them afterwards. And very well they do it, too! They gave us a capital one last year, about a field-mouse who was captured at sea by a Barbary corsair, and made to row in a galley; and when he escaped and got home again, his lady-love had gone into a convent. Here, you! You were in it, I remember. Get up and recite a bit.'

The field-mouse addressed got up on his legs, giggled shyly, looked round the room, and remained absolutely tongue-tied. His comrades cheered him on, Mole coaxed and encouraged him, and the Rat went so far as to take him by the shoulders and shake him; but nothing could overcome his stage-fright. They were all busily engaged on him like watermen applying the Royal Humane Society's regulations to a case of long submersion, when the latch clicked, the door opened, and the field-mouse with the lantern re-appeared, staggering under the weight of his basket.

There was no more talk of play-acting once the very real and solid contents of the basket had been tumbled out on the table. Under the generalship of Rat, everybody was set to do something or to fetch something. In a very few minutes supper was ready, and Mole, as he took the head of the table in a sort of dream, saw a lately barren board set thick with savoury comforts; saw his little friends' faces brighten and beam as they fell to without delay; and then let himself loose – for he was famished indeed – on the provender so magically provided, thinking what a happy home-coming this had turned out, after all. As they ate, they talked of old times, and the field-mice gave him the local gossip up to date, and answered as well as they could the hundred questions he had to ask them. The Rat said little or nothing, only taking care that each guest had what he wanted, and plenty of it, and that Mole had no trouble or anxiety about anything.

They clattered off at last, very grateful and showering wishes of the season, with their jacket pockets stuffed with remembrances for the small brothers and sisters at home. When the door had closed on the last of them and the chink of the lanterns had died away, Mole and Rat kicked the fire up, drew their chairs in, brewed themselves a last nightcap of mulled ale, and discussed the events of the long day. At last the Rat, with a tremendous yawn, said, 'Mole, old chap, I'm ready to drop. Sleepy is simply not the word. That your own bunk over on that side? Very well, then, I'll take this. What a ripping little house this is! Everything so handy!'

He clambered into his bunk and rolled himself well up in the blankets, and slumber gathered him forthwith, as a swath of barley is folded into the arms of the reaping-machine.

MEMORIES OF CHRISTMAS

Dylan Thomas

One Christmas was so much like another, in those years, around the sea town corner now, and out of all sound except the distant speaking of the voices I sometimes hear a moment before sleep, that I can never remember whether it snowed for six days and six nights when I was twelve or whether it snowed for twelve days and twelve nights when I was six; or whether the ice broke and the skating grocer vanished like a snowman through a white trap-door on that same Christmas Day that the mince-pies finished Uncle Arnold and we tobogganed down the seaward hill, all the afternoon, on the best tea-tray, and Mrs Griffiths complained, and we threw a snowball at her niece, and my hands burned so, with the heat and the cold, when I held them in front of the fire, that I cried for twenty minutes and then had some jelly.

All the Christmases roll down the hill towards the Welsh-speaking sea like a snowball growing whiter and bigger and rounder, like a cold and headlong moon bundling down the sky that was our street; and they stop at the rim of the ice-edged, fish-freezing waves, and I plunge my hands in the snow and bring out whatever I can find; holly or robins or pudding, squabbles and carols and oranges and tin whistles, and the fire in the front room, and bang go the crackers, and holy, holy, holy, ring the bells, and the glass bells shaking on the tree, and Mother Goose, and Struwelpeter – oh! the baby-burning flames and the clacking scissorman! – Billy Bunter and Black Beauty, Little Women and boys who have three helpings, Alice and Mrs Potter's badgers, penknives, teddy-bears – named after a Mr Theodore Bear, their inventor, or father, who died recently in the United States – mouth-organs, tin-soldiers, and blancmange, and Auntie Bessie playing 'Pop Goes the Weasel' and 'Nuts in May' and 'Oranges and Lemons' on the untuned piano in the parlour all through the thimble-hiding musical-chairing blind-man's-buffing party at the end of the never-to-be-forgotten day at the end of the unremembered year.

In goes my hand into that wool-white bell-tongued ball of holidays resting at the margin of the carol-singing sea, and out come Mrs Prothero and the firemen.

It was on the afternoon of the day of Christmas Eve, and I was in Mrs Prothero's garden, waiting for cats, with her son Jim. It was snowing. It was always snowing at Christmas; December, in my memory, is white as Lapland, though there were no reindeers. But there were cats. Patient, cold, and callous, our hands wrapped in socks, we waited to snowball the cats. Sleek and long as jaguars and terrible-whiskered, spitting and snarling they would slink and sidle over the white back-garden walls, and the lynx-eyed hunters, Jim and I, furcapped and moccasined trappers from Hudson's Bay off Eversley Road, would hurl our deadly snowballs at the green of their eyes. The wise cats never appeared. We were so still, Eskimo-footed arctic marksmen in the muffling silence of the eternal snows – eternal, ever since Wednesday – that we never heard Mrs Prothero's first cry from her igloo at the bottom of the garden. Or, if we heard it at all, it was, to us, like the far-off challenge of our enemy and prey, the neighbour's Polar Cat. But soon the voice grew louder. 'Fire!' cried Mrs Prothero, and she beat the dinner-gong. And we ran down the garden, with the snowballs in our arms, towards the house, and smoke, indeed, was pouring out of the dining-room, and the gong was bombilating, and Mrs Prothero was announcing ruin like a town-crier in Pompeii. This was better than all the cats in Wales standing on the wall in a row. We bounded into the house, laden with snowballs, and stopped at the open door of the smoke-filled room. Something was burning all right; perhaps it was Mr Prothero, who always slept there after midday dinner with a newspaper over his face; but he was standing in the middle of the room, saying 'A fine Christmas!' and smacking at the smoke with a slipper.

'Call the fire-brigade,' cried Mrs Prothero as she beat the gong.

'They won't be there,' said Mr Prothero, 'it's Christmas.'

There was no fire to be seen, only clouds of smoke and Mr Prothero standing in the middle of them, waving his slipper as though he were conducting.

'Do something,' he said.

And we threw all our snowballs into the smoke – I think we missed Mr Prothero – and ran out of the house to the telephone-box.

'Let's call the police as well,' Jim said.

'And the ambulance.'

'And Ernie Jenkins, he likes fires.'

But we only called the fire-brigade, and soon the fire-engine came and three tall men in helmets brought a hose into the house and Mr Prothero got out just in time before they turned it on. Nobody could have had a noisier Christmas Eve. And when the firemen turned off the hose and were standing in the wet and smoky room, Jim's aunt, Miss Prothero, came downstairs and peered in at them. Jim and I waited, very quietly, to hear what she would say to them. She said the right thing, always. She looked at the three tall firemen in their shining helmets, standing among the smoke and cinders and dissolving snowballs, and she said: 'Would you like something to read?'

Now out of that bright white snowball of Christmas gone comes the stocking, the stocking of stockings, that hung at the foot of the bed with the arm of a golliwog dangling over the top and small bells ringing in the toes. There was a company, gallant and scarlet but never nice to taste though I always tried when very young, of belted and busbied and musketed lead soldiers so soon to lose their heads and legs in the wars on the kitchen table after the tea-things, the mince-pies, and the cakes that I helped to make by stoning the raisins and eating them, had been cleared away; and a bag of moist and many-coloured jelly-babies and a folded flag and a false nose and a tram-conductor's cap and a machine that punched tickets and rang a bell; never a catapult; once, by a mistake that no one could explain, a little hatchet; and a rubber buffalo, or it may have been a horse, with a yellow head and haphazard legs; and a celluloid duck that made, when you pressed it, a most unducklike noise, a mewing moo that an ambitious cat might make who wishes to be a cow; and a painting-book in which I could make the grass, the trees, the sea, and the animals any colour I pleased: and still the dazzling sky-blue sheep are grazing in the red field under a flight of rainbow-beaked and pea-green birds.

Christmas morning was always over before you could say Jack Frost. And look! suddenly the pudding was burning! Bang the gong and call the fire-brigade and the book-loving firemen! Someone found the silver three-penny-bit with a currant on it; and the someone was always Uncle Arnold. The motto in my cracker read:

Let's all have fun this Christmas Day,

Let's play and sing and shout hooray!

and the grown-ups turned their eyes towards the ceiling, and Auntie Bessie, who had already been frightened, twice, by a clockwork mouse, whimpered at the sideboard and had some elderberry wine. And someone put a glass bowl full of nuts on the littered table, and my uncle said, as he said once every year: 'I've got a shoe-nut here. Fetch me a shoe-horn to open it, boy.'

And dinner was ended.

And I remember that on the afternoon of Christmas Day, when the others sat around the fire and told each other that this was nothing, no, nothing, to the great snowbound and turkey-proud yule-log-crackling holly-berry-bedizined and kissing-under-the-mistletoe Christmas when *they* were children. I would go out, school-capped and gloved and mufflered, with my bright new boots squeaking, into the white world on to the seaward hill, to call on Jim and Dan and Jack and to walk with them through the silent snowscape of our town.

We went padding through the streets, leaving huge deep footprints in the snow, on the hidden pavements.

'I bet people'll think there's been hippoes.'

'What would you do if you saw a hippo coming down Terrace Road?'

'I'd go like this, bang! I'd throw him over the railings and roll him down the hill and then I'd tickle him under the ear and he'd wag his tail...'

'What would you do if you saw *two* hippoes...?'

Iron-flanked and bellowing he-hippoes clanked and blundered and battered through the scudding snow towards us as we passed by Mr Daniel's house.

'Let's post Mr Daniel a snowball through his letter-box.'

'Let's write things in the snow.'

'Let's write "Mr Daniel looks like a spaniel" all over his lawn.'

'Look,' Jack said, 'I'm eating snow-pie.'

'What's it taste like?'

'Like snow-pie,' Jack said.

Or we walked on the white shore.

'Can the fishes see it's snowing?'

'They think it's the sky falling down.'

The silent one-clouded heavens drifted on to the sea.

'All the old dogs have gone.'

Dogs of a hundred mingled makes yapped in the summer at the sea-rim and yelped at the trespassing mountains of the waves.

'I bet St Bernards would like it now.'

And we were snowblind travellers lost on the north hills, and the great dewlapped dogs, with brandy-flasks round their necks, ambled and shambled up to us, baying 'Excelsior'.

We returned home through the desolate poor sea-facing streets where only a few children fumbled with bare red fingers in the thick wheel-rutted snow and cat-called after us, their voices fading away, as we trudged uphill, into the cries of the dock-birds and the hooters of ships out in the white and whirling bay.

Bring out the tall tales now that we told by the fire as we roasted chestnuts and the gaslight bubbled low. Ghosts with their heads under their arms trailed their chains and said 'whooo' like owls in the long nights when I dared not look over my shoulder; wild beasts lurked in the cubby-hole under the stairs where the gas-meter ticked. 'Once upon a time,' Jim said, 'there were three boys, just like us, who got lost in the dark in the snow, near Bethesda Chapel, and this is what happened to them...' It was the most dreadful happening I had ever heard.

And I remember that we went singing carols once, a night or two before Christmas Eve, when there wasn't the shaving of a moon to light the secret,

white-flying streets. At the end of a long road was a drive that led to a large house, and we stumbled up the darkness of the drive that night, each one of us afraid, each one holding a stone in his hand in case, and all of us too brave to say a word. The wind made through the drive-trees noises as of old and unpleasant and maybe web-footed men wheezing in caves. We reached the black bulk of the house.

'What shall we give them?' Dan whispered.

'"Hark the Herald"? "Christmas comes but Once a Year"?'

'No,' Jack said: 'We'll sing "Good King Wenceslas". I'll count three.'

One, two, three, and we began to sing, our voices high and seemingly distant in the snow-felted darkness round the house that was occupied by nobody we knew. We stood close together, near the dark door.

Good King Wenceslas looked out

On the Feast of Stephen.

And then a small, dry voice, like the voice of someone who has not spoken for a long time, suddenly joined our singing: a small, dry voice from the other side of the door: a small, dry voice through the keyhole. And when we stopped running we were outside *our* house; the front room was lovely and bright.

SNOW IN THE SUBURBS

Thomas Hardy

Every branch big with it,
Bent every twig with it;
Every fork like a white web-foot;
Every street and pavement mute:
Some flakes have lost their way, and grope back upward, when
Meeting those meandering down they turn and descend again.

The palings are glued together like a wall,
And there is no waft of wind with the fleecy fall.

A sparrow enters the tree,
Whereon immediately
A snow-lump thrice his own slight size
Descends on him and showers his head and eyes,
And overturns him,
And near inurns him,
And lights on a nether twig, when its brush
Starts off a volley of other lodging lumps with a rush.

The steps are a blanched slope,
Up which, with feeble hope,
A black cat comes, wide-eyed and thin;
And we take him in.

JERRY'S NEW YEAR

Extract from *Black Beauty*
Anna Sewell

Christmas and the New Year are very merry times for some people; but for cabmen and cabmen's horses these times are no holiday, though they may be a harvest. There are so many parties, balls, and places of amusement open that the work is hard and often late. Sometimes driver and horse, shivering with cold, have to wait for hours in the rain or frost, whilst the merry people within are dancing to the music. I wonder if the beautiful ladies ever think of the weary cabman waiting on his box, and of his patient beast standing till his legs get stiff with cold!

I had now most of the evening work as I was well accustomed to standing, and Jerry was also more afraid of Hotspur, the new horse, taking cold. We had a great deal of late work in the Christmas week, and Jerry's cough was bad, but, however late we were, Polly sat up for him, and, looking anxious troubled, she came out with the lantern to meet him.

On the evening of the New Year we had to take two gentlemen to a house in one of the West End squares. We sat them down at nine o'clock, and were told to come again at eleven. "But," said one of them, "as it is a card party, you may have to wait a few minutes, but don't be late."

As the clock struck eleven we were at the door, for Jerry was always punctual. The clock chimed the quarters – one, two, three, and then struck twelve; but the door did not open.

The wind had been very changeable, with squalls of rain during the day, but now it came on sharp, driving sleet, which seemed to come all the way round one; it was very cold, and there was no shelter. Jerry got off his box and came and pulled one of my cloths a little more over my neck; then, stamping his feet, he took a turn up and down, then began to beat his arms, and that set him on coughing; so he opened the cab door and sat at the bottom with his feet on the pavement, and was thus a little sheltered. Still the clock chimed the quarters, but no one came. At half-past twelve he rang the bell, and asked the servant if he would be wanted that night.

'Oh! yes, you'll be wanted safe enough,' said the man; 'you must not go, it will soon be over.' And again Jerry sat down, but his voice was so hoarse I could hardly hear him.

At a quarter past one the door opened, and the two gentlemen came out; they got into the cab without a word, and told Jerry where to drive; it was nearly two miles away. My legs were numb with cold, and I thought I should have stumbled. When the men got out, they never said they were sorry to have kept us waiting so long, but were angry at the charge. However, as Jerry never charged more than was his due, he never took less, and so they had to pay for the two hours and a quarter of waiting but it was hard-earned money to Jerry.

At last we got home. He could hardly speak, and his cough was dreadful. Polly asked no questions, but opened the door and held the lantern for him.

'Can't I do something?' she said.

'Yes; get Jack something warm, and then boil me some gruel.'

This was said in a hoarse whisper. He could hardly get his breath, but he gave me a rub down as usual, and even went up into the hayloft for an extra bundle of straw for my bed. Polly brought me a warm mash that made me comfortable; and then they locked the door.

It was late the next morning before anyone came, and then it was only Harry. He cleaned and fed us, and swept out the stalls; then he put the straw back again as if it was Sunday. He was very still, and neither whistled nor sang. At noon he came again and gave us our food and water: this time Dolly came with him. She was crying, and I could gather from what they said that Jerry was dangerously ill, and the doctor said it was a bad case. So two days passed, and there was great trouble indoors. We saw only Harry and sometimes Dolly. I think she came for company, for Polly was always with Jerry, who had to be kept very quiet.

On the third day, whilst Harry was in the stable, a tap came at the door, and Governor Grant came in.

'I wouldn't go to the house, my boy,' he said, 'but I want to know how your father is.'

'He is very bad,' said Harry, 'he can't be much worse. They call it bronchitis, and the doctor thinks it will turn one way or another tonight.'

'That's bad, very bad,' said Grant, shaking his head. 'I know two men who died of that last week. It takes 'em off in no time; but whilst there's life there's hope, so you must keep up your spirits.'

'Yes,' said Harry quickly, 'and the doctor said that father had a better chance than most men, because he didn't drink. He said yesterday the fever was so high that if father had been a drinking man, it would have burnt him up like a piece of paper; but I believe he thinks he will get over it; don't you think he will, Mr. Grant?'

The Governor looked puzzled.

'If there's any rule that good men should get over these things, I am sure he will, my boy. He's the best man I know. I'll look in early to-morrow.'

Early next morning he was there.

'Well?' said he.

'Father is better,' said Harry. 'Mother hopes he will get over it.'

'Thank God!' said the Governor; 'and now you must keep him warm, and

---

keep his mind easy. And that brings me to the horses. You see, Jack will be all the better for the rest of a week or two in a warm stable, and you can easily take him a turn up and down the street to stretch his legs; but this young one, if he does not get work, will soon be all up on end as you may say, and will be rather too much for you; and when he does go out, there'll be an accident.'

'He is like that now,' said Harry; 'I have kept him short of corn, but he's so full of spirit I don't know what to do with him.'

'Just so,' said Grant. 'Now look here. Will you tell your mother that, if she is agreeable, I will come for him every day till something is arranged, and take him for a good spell of work; and whatever he earns, I'll bring your mother half of it, and that will help with the horses' feed. Your father is in a good club, I know, but that won't keep the horses, and they'll be eating their heads off all this time: I'll come at noon to hear what she says'; and without waiting for Harry's thanks, he was gone.

At noon I think he went and saw Polly, for Harry and he came to the stable together, harnessed Hotspur, and took him out.

For a week or more he came for Hotspur, and when Harry thanked him or said anything about his kindness, he laughed it off, saying, it was all good luck for him, for his horses were wanting a little rest which they could not otherwise have had.

Jerry steadily grew better, but the doctor said that he must never go back to the cab-work again if he wished to be an old man. The children had many consultations together about what father and mother would do, and how they could help to earn money.

One afternoon Hotspur was brought in very wet and dirty.

'The streets are nothing but slush,' said the Governor; 'it will give you a good warming, my boy, to get him clean and dry.'

'All right, Governor,' said Harry, 'I shall not leave him till he is; you know I have been trained by my father.'

'I wish all the boys had been trained like you,' said the Governor.

While Harry was sponging off the mud from Hotspur's body and legs, Dolly came in, looking very full of something.

'Who lives at Fairstowe, Harry? Mother has got a letter from Fairstowe; she seemed so glad, and ran upstairs to father with it.'

'Don't you know? Why, it is the name of Mrs Fowler's place – mother's old mistress, you know – the lady that father met last summer, who sent you and me five shillings each.'

'Oh! Mrs. Fowler; of course I know all about her. I wonder what she is writing to mother about.'

'Mother wrote to her last week,' said Harry. 'You know she told father if ever he gave up the cab-work, she would like to know. I wonder what she says; run in and see, Dolly.'

Harry scrubbed away at Hotspur with a 'huish! huish!' like any old ostler.

In a few minutes Dolly came dancing into the stable.

'Oh, Harry! was there ever anything so beautiful? Mrs Fowler says we are all to go and live near her. There is a cottage now empty that will just suit us, with a garden, a hen-house, apple-trees, and everything! Her coachman is going away in the spring, and then she will want father in his place. And there are good families round, where you can get a place in the garden or stable, or as a page-boy; and there's a good school for me. Mother is laughing and crying by turns, and father does look so happy!'

'That's uncommon jolly,' said Harry, 'and just the right thing, I should say. It will suit father and mother both; but I don't intend to be a page-boy with tight clothes and rows of buttons. I'll be a groom or a gardener.'

It was quickly settled that, as soon as Jerry was well enough, they should remove to the country, and that the cab and horses should be sold as soon as possible.

This was heavy news for me, for I was not young now, and could not look for any improvement in my condition. Since I left Birtwick I had never been so happy as with my dear master, Jerry; but three years of cab-work, even under the best conditions, will tell on one's strength, and I felt that I was not the horse that I had been.

Grant said at once that he would take Hotspur. There were men on the stand who would have bought me; but Jerry said I should not go to cab-work again with just anybody, and the Governor promised to find a place for me where I should be comfortable.

The day came for going away. Jerry had not been allowed to go out yet, and I never saw him after that New Year's Eve. Polly and the children came to bid me goodbye. 'Poor old Jack! dear old Jack! I wish we could take you with us,' she said; and then, laying her hand on my mane, she put her face close to my neck and kissed me. Dolly was crying, and she kissed me too. Harry stroked me a great deal, but said nothing, only he seemed very sad; and so I was led away to my new place.

Ring Out Wild Bells

Extract from *In Memoriam*
Alfred, Lord Tennyson

Ring out wild bells to the wild sky,
The flying cloud, the frosty light:
The year is dying in the night;
Ring out, wild bells, and let him die.

Ring out the old, ring in the new,
Ring, happy bells, across the snow:
The year is going, let him go;
Ring out the false, ring in the true.

Auld Lang Syne

Robert Burns

Chorus: For auld lang syne, my dear,

For auld lang syne,   *days of long ago*

We'll tak a cup o kindness yet,

For auld lang syne!

Should auld acquaintance be forgot,

And never brought to mind?

Should auld acquaintance be forgot,

And auld lang syne?

And surely ye'll be your pint-stowp,   *pay for*

And surely I'll be mine,

And we'll tak a cup o kindness yet,

For auld lang syne!

We twa hae run about the braes,   *hillsides*

And pon'd the gowans fire,   *pulled/wild daisies*

But we've wander'd monie a weary fit,   *many/foot*

Sin auld lang syne.

We twa hae paidl'd in the burn   *waded*

Frae morning sun till dine,   *dinner-time*

But seas between us braid hae roar'd   *broad*

Sin auld lang syne.

And there's a hand my trusty fiere,   *chum*

And gie's a hand o thine,   *give us*

And we'll tak a right guid-willie waught,   *good will draught*

For auld lang syne.

AFTERWORD

Now it is New Year's Eve. The Christmas tree still shines across the harbour and has been joined by the lights of three ships sheltering in the bay from a mid-winter gale. They ride on their anchors and turn with the tide.

At one state of the tide, the three ships turn bow-first towards our house and look, then, like three giant Christmas trees swaying on a sea of diamonds.

So, here we are, at the turn of the tide, the turn of the year, the turn of the Century and, even with the Millennium, the turn of a thousand years. Really, it is the turn of two thousand years, since that first Christmas star hung as a sign in the night.

And that is the story that will still be told a thousand years from now.

ACKNOWLEDGMENTS

p15 *Picture-Books in Winter*. Illustrations from Michael Foreman's *A Child's Garden of Verses* © Michael Foreman. Reproduced by permission of the publisher Penguin UK. p16 The Twelve Days of Christmas. Illustrations from Michael Foreman's *Mother Goose* © 1991 Michael Foreman. Foreword © 1991 Iona Opic. Reproduced by permission of the publisher Walker Books Ltd., London. p31 *The Boy at the Window* by Richard Wilbur. Reproduced by permission of the publisher Faber & Faber, London. p39 'Carols in Gloucestershire' from *Cider with Rosie* by Laurie Lee, reprinted by permission of Hogarth Press. p52 *Winter Morning* copyright © 1962 by Ogden Nash. Reprinted by permission of Curtis Brown, Ltd. New York. p61 *The Christmas Story*. Extracts from the Authorized Version of the Bible (The King James Bible), the rights in which are vested in the Crown, are reproduced by permission of the Crown's Patentee, Cambridge University Press. p67 *A Christmas Carol* by G. K. Chesterton, reprinted by permission of A.P. Watt Ltd on behalf of The Royal Literary Fund. Illustrations from Michael Foreman's *A Christmas Carol* © Michael Foreman, published by Penguin UK and reproduced by permission of the publisher. p68 'Stopping by Woods on a Snowy Evening' from *The Poetry of Robert Frost*, originally published by Jonathan Cape, reproduced by permission of the Estate of Robert Frost, the editor, Edward Connery Latham, and Jonathan Cape. p69 *The Night Before Christmas*. Illustrations © by Michael Foreman. Reproduced by permission of the publisher Intervisual Books, Inc. p92 *Cowboy Carol* by Cecil Broadhurst © 1949 The Oxford Group, 24 Greencoat, London SW1P 1DX. p94 'Outdoor Song' from *The House of Pooh Corner* © A. A. Milne. Copyright under the Berne Convention. Published by Methuen, an imprint of Egmont Children's Books Limited, London and used with permission. p104 *Memories of Christmas* by Dylan Thomas, published by JM Dent, reprinted by permission of David Higham Associates.